FLY GUY AND THE FRANKENFLY

Tedd Arnold

Cartwheel Books

An Imprint of Scholastic Inc.

Specially for Owen and Kei!

Library of Congress Cataloging-in-Publication Data

Arnold, Tedd.
Fly Guy and the Frankenfly / Tedd Arnold. -- 1st ed.
p. cm. -- (Fly guy ; #13)
Summary: Buzz has a nightmare that his best friend Fly Guy has created a gigantic Frankenfly monster.
ISBN 978-0-545-49328-4
1. Flies--Juvenile fiction. 2. Monsters--Juvenile fiction. 3. Nightmares--Juvenile fiction. 4. Best friends--Juvenile fiction. [1. Flies--Fiction. 2. Monsters--Fiction. 3. Nightmares--Fiction. 4. Best friends--Fiction.] I. Title. II. Series: Arnold, Tedd. Fly Guy ; #13.

PZ7.A7379Fkm 2013
813.54--dc23

2012043724

ISBN 978-0-545-49328-4

10 9 8 7 6   14 15 16 17

Printed in China 38
First edition, July 2013

A boy had a pet fly.
He named him Fly Guy.
And Fly Guy could
say the boy's name—

BUZZ!

Chapter 1

It was a dark and stormy night. Buzz and Fly Guy were playing.

Buzz made puzzles
for both of them.

Buzz made costumes
for both of them.

Buzz made a drawing
for both of them.

Finally, Buzz said,
"Time for bed, Fly Guy."

Fly Guy said,

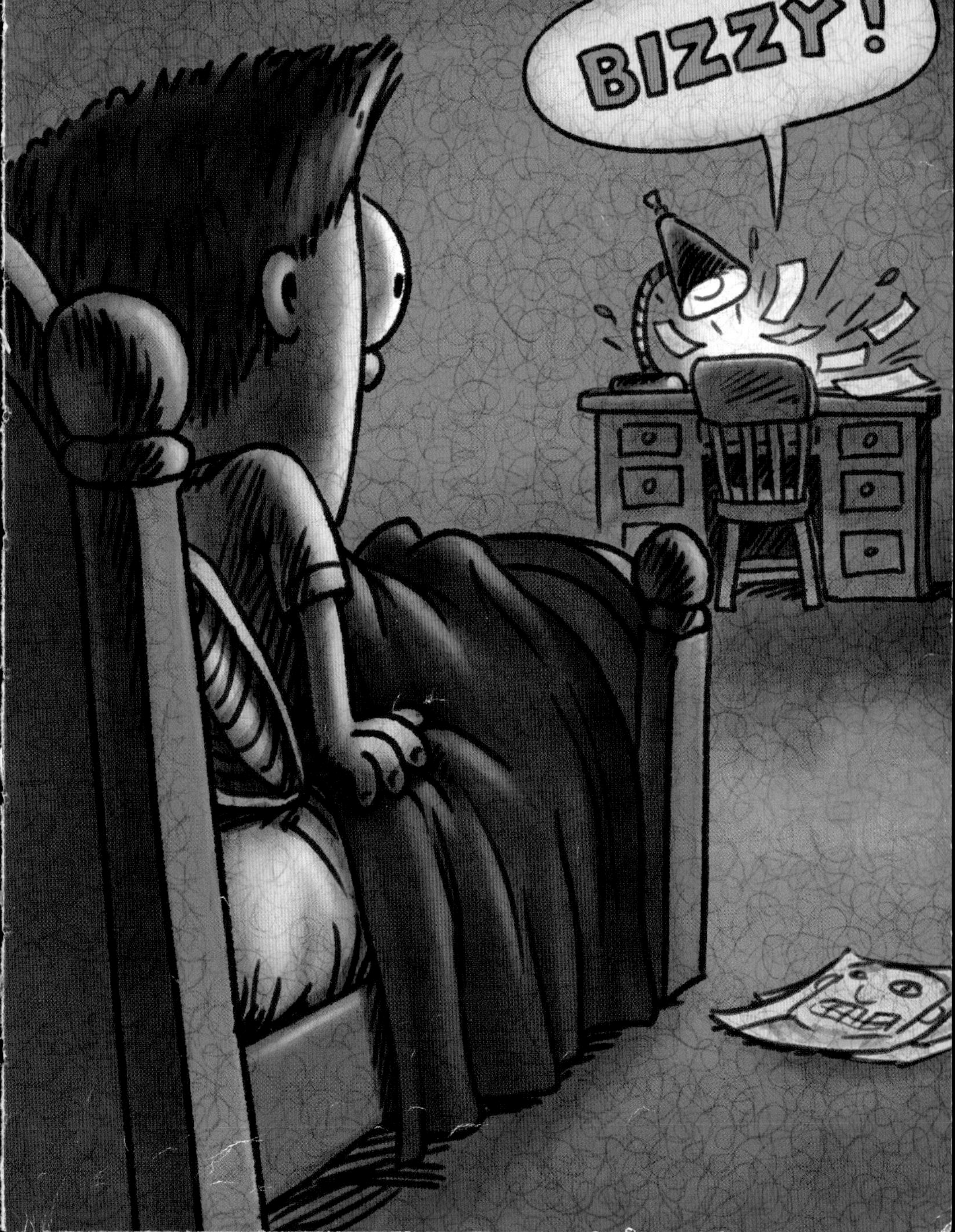

As Buzz fell asleep,
he wondered, "What
is Fly Guy making?"

Chapter 2

Late that night a strange
light woke up Buzz.

Fly Guy was making
something in his laboratory.

He was making a monster!

Fly Guy turned on the power.
The monster sat up.

Buzz cried, "It's Frankenfly!"

Frankenfly heard Buzz.
He stood up.

He walked to the bed.

Frankenfly picked up Buzz.

Fly Guy yelled,

Fly Guy shut off the power.

CRASH!

Frankenfly dropped Buzz
and fell onto the bed.

Chapter 3

Buzz fell out of bed and
woke up. It was morning.

CRASH

"Wow!" said Buzz. "That was a *bad* dream."

Fly Guy was not in his bed.

He was asleep on the desk.

"Fly Guy," said Buzz, "did you make something last night?"

Fly Guy said,

"You made me?" asked Buzz.

"YEZZZ!" said Fly Guy.

He pointed to a piece of paper.

"It's me!" said Buzz.

"It's a painting of you
and me!" said Buzz.

"How did you paint this? My
brushes are too big for you."

Buzz said, "We are the BEST best friends ever!"